PESTO PIZZA MURDER

THE PAPA PACELLI'S PIZZERIA SERIES BOOK 31

PATTI BENNING

SUMMER PRESCOTT BOOKS PUBLISHING

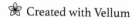

CHAPTER ONE

One lonely suitcase sat in the middle of the queen-sized bed. It was half-full of clothes, and Russell Ward was still adding more. Eleanora Ward sat on the wooden stool at her vanity, watching her husband pack with her arms crossed in front of her.

"Don't forget your razor," she commented as he stepped into the bathroom with his toiletry bag. "Last time you forgot it, you used one of the hotel ones and got razor burn. And don't forget to bring your laptop so we can video call each other. And don't forget —"

"Ellie." Russell poked his head out of the bathroom. "Are you sure you don't want me to stay home?"

She looked down at the top of her vanity, an antique that her grandmother had insisted that she take with her when she and her husband bought their new home. For a moment, she imagined telling Russell that yes, she wanted him to stay, that she would be lonely when he left, that she didn't feel at home in their new house yet and with strangers renting her grandmother's home next door, she couldn't even go there for comfort.

Instead, she sighed then looked up and met her husband's eyes. "I want you to go. I know how much you enjoy these conferences, and I know how much you learn at them. I travel down to Florida all the time, it wouldn't be fair for me to ask you not to go to this."

"A police conference is different than you running down to Florida to manage the second pizzeria," he said, coming fully out of the bathroom. "I'm serious, Ellie, I don't have to go. If you want me to stay here, I will. You've been on edge all morning, and I get the feeling you'd rather I stayed."

"I'm going to miss you," she admitted. "But I know this will be good for you. You almost never get time off work, and it would be selfish of me to ask you to stay. I just... I don't know, I have a bad feeling about this trip. The weather is supposed to be terrible all along the coast, and I'm worried about you flying out. Plus, I think I'm still shaken up about what happened to your cousin. Being here alone makes me feel weird, and I'm not usually the superstitious sort."

"I can still cancel my ticket..." he began.

Ellie shook her head. "*No.* You should go. I'll be fine, I'm just trying to explain why I've been so out of sorts all morning. I promise, I'll be all right here, Russell."

He frowned. "Are you sure you can't come with me?"

"I need to be here at the pizzeria. We've got a huge meat shipment coming in from a new supplier, and if something goes wrong with it and I'm three states away, it won't be good. Just call me as soon as your plane gets in, all right?"

"Of course." He walked over to give her a kiss on the cheek. "And remember, you can always go over to Shannon and James' house if you need the company. James said to tell you you're welcome to eat dinner with them every night, if you want. I know it's going to be lonely out here, especially since your grandmother's in Florida. Promise me you'll have dinner with them at least a couple of times, all right? I hate to think of you eating here alone every night."

"I promise," she said. "I know I'll go stir crazy if I don't do anything but go to work and come home all week. Living alone out here is very different from living alone in the middle of Chicago. Don't get me wrong; I love where we live, but when you're gone and I'm alone here, it feels like I could be the only person in the entire world."

"I'll be just a phone call away. I'm sorry I'm leaving so soon after what happened with Bea, but I'll be back before you know it."

"I know." She gave him a smile, then stood up. "I'm going to go check the dryer to see if it's done. We need to get you packed and get on the road. The plane won't wait for anyone, not even a sheriff."

Two hours later, Ellie pulled away from the Portland, Maine airport with a tight feeling in her chest. Her husband going away for a week wouldn't usually bother her this much, but between the threatening weather and the intensity of the past few weeks while Russell grieved for the loss of a family member, she wasn't at all eager to have the time to herself. The thought of going back to an empty house, sitting in front of the TV, then going to bed alone was depressing.

I should treat myself, she thought. *Live it up tonight, then start eating healthier again tomorrow.* She smiled, remembering the new Thai food restaurant in Benton Harbor that had opened only a couple months ago. She had just enough time to call in an order and pick it up on her way back home. Russell might not be there, but she still had the dogs and Marlowe, the greenwing macaw, to keep her company. With the thought of as much Thai food as she could eat and Sawyer and Bunny snuggled up to her on the couch while she re-watched one of her favorite romantic comedies, the evening suddenly seemed a lot less bleak. She would get through this week just fine, she just had to re-learn how to enjoy spending time with herself again.

CHAPTER TWO

The next morning, Ellie woke up sprawled out on her bed, with Bunny, her papillon, curled up on the pillow next to her head. *One advantage of sleeping alone is that I can take up as much space as I want*, she thought, stretching luxuriously before glancing at the clock by her bed. When she saw the time, she frowned. It was almost eight, but the light that was creeping its way into the room around the curtains was weak enough that she had thought it was much earlier.

She got up, nearly tripping over Sawyer, who was snoring on the floor next to the bed, and pulled back the curtains. Outside, a sky full of dark, menacing clouds greeted her. She felt a cold feeling in the pit of her stomach. Winter was almost over, but in northern Maine, that never meant much. Snow storms had been predicted for the next week, and by the look of the clouds outside, they were due for a bad one sometime today. It wasn't snowing yet, but she knew that it could start at any time. Already, she could hear the wind whistling around the house's eaves, and an involuntary shiver worked its way down her spine at the eerie noise.

She and Russell had bought the house only a few short months ago. They had gotten a killer price on it due to the house's history. At the time, the knowledge of the multiple deaths that had occurred inside the house hadn't bothered her much, but now, alone for the next week right after yet another death had been added to the count, she was beginning to feel uneasy with every creak and groan the house made. The fact that she didn't believe in ghosts didn't seem to help calm her jumpy nerves at all.

"I need coffee," she said out loud, closing the curtains with more force than was necessary. A winter storm was the last thing she needed. It would take a bucket full of good luck for the house to keep from losing power once the snow hit.

As she made her way downstairs, the dogs running ahead of her, she considered closing the pizzeria for the day, but it wasn't snowing *yet*, and she was looking forward to the familiar, comforting warmth of the pizzeria's kitchen. *I can always close early if the storm gets really bad*, she thought. *I don't want Pete and Iris to have to do deliveries if it's snowing heavily. The roads always get bad more quickly than I expect.*

She hit the button on the coffee pot to start the drink brewing before opening the back door to let the dogs out. A blast of wind caught the door and nearly slammed it into her face before she braced herself. Grumbling, she shooed Sawyer outside, then turned to look for Bunny. The little Papillon was standing a few feet back, giving her a pitiful look.

"You have to go out," Ellie said apologetically. "I

know it's terrible out there, but if you just go do your business and come right back in, it won't be too bad."

It took another few seconds of convincing, but at last the little dog slunk outside, her tail between her legs. Ellie made a mental note to start keeping Bunny's sweater by the back door. The weather was supposed to be bad all week, and she didn't blame the papillon for being reluctant to go out in it.

Even Sawyer didn't want to be outside in the blowing wind for any longer than necessary, and it wasn't long before she cracked open the door to let the two chilled dogs back into the house. She filled their food bowls before pouring herself a cup of coffee, then took a seat at the kitchen island while she sipped the drink, slowly waking up.

One thing she loved about her job was that there were no early mornings. She still had a good hour before she had to start getting ready for work, and enjoyed the fact that she didn't have to rush.

However, this morning wasn't meant for kicking her feet up and relaxing. She was going to be gone until late that evening, and if the storm knocked the power out before she got back, then the animals would be relying on the backup generator to kick on to keep them warm.

The generator had been Russell's idea. They usually lost power at least twice, if not more, each winter, sometimes for spans of almost a week. While a short outage wasn't the end of the world for them or the dogs, a longer one ran the risk of having the pipes freeze and burst, and Marlowe wasn't anywhere near as hardy as the rest of them when it came to low temperatures. The generator they had purchased didn't hold more than a day's worth of fuel, but it would come on automatically if there was an outage and could be refilled with regular gasoline.

She spent the morning double checking the generator and then touching base with Russell. She could tell over their video call how happy he seemed, and didn't want to wreck his mood by mentioning her worry over the coming storm. It lifted her heart to hear him talk excitedly about the speakers he would get to hear at the police conference that day, and when they said their goodbyes, she was able to shut her laptop with a genuine smile on her face.

Thankfully the clouds held their snow in for the morning, and the roads were clear as she drove to town, even if the sky was still ominous and dark. When she let herself in to the pizzeria, she felt an immediate sense of calm come over her. The familiar scents and sights, the hum of the fridge and freezer, even the forgotten pair of gloves someone had left on the staff table all felt like home here. There were no ghosts, real or imaginary, here.

She went through her usual morning routine, turning on the ovens to pre-heat, setting the radio to her favorite station, and doing a final check of the dining area to make sure it was ready for opening.

Then, she washed her hands and got to work making the fresh marinara sauce for that day's pizzas.

It didn't take her long to get the sauce simmering and the crusts for the pepperoni and cheese pizzas that they served by the slice pre-cooking in the oven. Once everything was on track for that, she turned her attention to making the week's special; chicken pesto on Papa Pacelli's famous thin crust pizza.

While the marinara sauce was made fresh daily, she had made the pesto two days before. She always thought the flavor was better after it had had a day or two to sit, and she was determined to take as few shortcuts as possible when it came to the food she served. Her pizzeria was one of the best in the state, and she knew that she had to keep re-earning that title daily.

The pesto sauce might have been made already, but the chicken needed to be cooked, the onions sliced, and the cheese grated. She hummed to herself as she worked, moving easily around the kitchen. She knew it even better than the kitchen at home, and the thought made her smile. Sometimes she was surprised by how much she just *loved* the pizzeria. It meant the world to her, in a way no other job ever had. Sure, it wasn't glamorous, and she would never get to be a millionaire from it, but it was satisfying, meaningful work, and she enjoyed almost every second of it.

By the time the three by-the-slice pizzas were under the warming lights and ready to go, it was time to open for the day. She turned on the open sign and unlocked the door, taking a moment to frown through the front window. It still wasn't snowing, but the sky was even darker than before. If she craned her neck, she could just see the water in the marina down the road. The bay was steel-grey and choppy, with white spray flying up feet into the air.

She shivered and turned away from the window, back to her warm, comforting restaurant.

CHAPTER THREE

Despite, or maybe because of, the intimidating weather outside, the morning was unusually busy. Ellie cooked pizza after pizza for her customers, most of them to-go. It seemed like half the town wanted an easy, warm meal to feast on as a way to brace themselves against the harsh wind and impending snow. She couldn't blame them; there was something about winter weather that made her want to eat food laden with carbs and fat. She could understand why bears hibernated in the winter, and thought it was a shame that people didn't have that option.

She was glad for the backup when Iris and Pete arrived. They didn't start offering deliveries until mid-afternoon, but by the time Pete arrived and started taking pizzas out, they had a long list of orders to fill. Ellie knew the townspeople wanted their food delivered before the snow inevitably closed the roads. The whole town, it seemed, was getting ready for the blizzard that was sure to come.

By the time her employees arrived, Ellie was glad for the chance to take a break from cooking and sit at the register. Being on her feet all day made her legs ache, and sitting at the stool behind the front counter was a momentary bliss.

By now, snow had begun falling lightly outside, just a hint of what was to come. The dining room was quiet, with only one eat-in patron sitting near the door. Between answering the phone for delivery and pick-up orders, Ellie read through the report Linda had sent her about the Florida pizzeria. Seeing the projected profits for the next few months made her smile. Opening the second pizzeria had been a lot of work, but it had been more than worth it. *And it gives me an excuse to head down south when I get sick of the snow*, she thought, glancing outside. Just as she looked up, the front door opened, letting in three new customers. Two of them made their way to a booth, while the third made a beeline for the counter. She pulled her hood down and shook out her curly brown hair, unzipping her coat to reveal a black skirt and blouse underneath.

"Can we get a large chicken pesto pizza?" she asked, after a glance at the menu. "And three drinks from the cooler."

"Sure thing," Ellie said, smiling. "Will that be for here or to go?"

"For here. On second thought, can I also get a personal sized cheese pizza to go? I'm staying at a motel, and by the looks of things, I won't want to head out into town for anything else to eat."

"You probably won't," Ellie agreed. "I've got one large

pesto chicken pizza for here, and a personal sized cheese pizza to go, plus three drinks from the fridge. Will that be all?"

The other woman nodded and reached into her purse for her wallet. Ellie punched in the order, then reached across the counter to take the card. As she did so, she met the woman's eyes and saw that they were red and puffy, as if she had been crying.

Ellie ran the card and printed out the receipt, then handed both items to the woman. Unable to help herself, she asked, "Sorry if I'm being rude, but is everything all right? You look upset."

"I'm a mess, aren't I?" The woman gave a dry chuckle as she put the wallet back into her purse. "My brothers and I just left our mom's funeral."

"I'm so sorry," Ellie said. "Forget I said anything. My condolences to you and your brothers. Feel free to take as long as you need here, and I'll make sure no one interrupts you."

"Thanks." She gave Ellie a small smile. "My name's Jessie, by the way. Mark and I are from out of town, but Iggy's lived here for a while and he convinced us this was the best place to go for a quick, good meal and a chance to talk. It sounds like he was right about how nice everyone is here. I'm only going to be here for a few more days, until after my mother's will is read, but I love pizza, so I'll probably stop by at least once more if it's as good as my little brother tells me it is."

"Well, I hope we live up to your expectations," she replied. "I'll go run your order back. Feel free to grab your drinks. I'll get the pizza out to you as soon as possible."

True to her word, she kept an eye on the three mourning siblings and made sure nothing disturbed them. She wished there was more she could do. She knew how difficult losses like theirs could be, and felt her heart ache in sympathy.

As darkness fell, the pizzeria began to get more and more delivery orders. It still had yet to start snowing in earnest, and Pete and Iris did their best to keep up with the flurry of deliveries. By the time closing time came around, everyone was exhausted. Ellie had just enough presence of mind to make a personal pizza for herself before locking up and heading home.

The wind was even worse on the drive back, but she was beginning to hope that the promised snow wouldn't come. Though the sky had remained dark and ominous all day, they hadn't gotten anything more than flurries. The roads were still drivable, and none of her customers had complained about losing power. Her fingers were crossed that by morning the storm would have blown over, to deposit its load of snow elsewhere.

Her phone rang as she was unlocking her front door,

and by the time she had the door shut behind her and was able to dig through her purse, she had missed the call. Turning on the phone, she saw that the missed call was from Shannon. She paused to take off her shoes and shrug off her coat, then redialed the number, walking into the kitchen with her pizza and purse in her arms.

"Hey," Shannon said, answering the call. "Are you still in town?"

"Just got home," Ellie said. "What's going on?"

"I was wondering if you wanted to come over. James is staying at a hotel tonight; I told him not to risk driving home through the storm, but of course we're still waiting on all of that snow. It's lonely here, with just me and the baby. I was thinking of seeing if Joanna wanted to come over as well, and the three of us could watch a movie and have a girls' night in. But if you just got home, you probably don't want to turn around and drive back to town."

"I wouldn't mind too much, but I'd be worried about getting stuck there if the snow comes after all. With Russell out of town, I can't risk not being able to make it back here. The animals will need me to take care of them."

"Oh, that's right," Shannon said. "Sorry, I didn't even think of that."

"If you want, you and Andrew are more than welcome to come out here. And Joanna too, if you still want to call her." Ellie smiled, tucking the phone between her ear and shoulder as she opened the back door to let the dogs out. "A girls' night in sounds great to me, and there's plenty of space here if it ends up snowing and you don't want to drive home."

"If you're sure you don't mind, I'd love to come over."

"My plan was to eat alone in front of the TV tonight," Ellie replied with a chuckle. "Trust me, the company will be welcome."

"Great. I'll pack up Andrew's things and call Joanna to see if she wants to join us. I'll be there in about an hour."

"I'll put together some snacks and find us a movie to watch," Ellie said. "My night just got a whole lot better."

CHAPTER FOUR

With two of her closest friends and her little nephew in the house, things suddenly became much livelier. They set up Andrew's play pen in the corner of the living room, then Joanna and Shannon looked through the DVDs while Ellie put the finishing touches on a plate of meat and cheese and took a pan of brownies out of the oven. Deciding they might as well live it up a little, she opened a bottle of wine she and Russell had gotten for their wedding. None of them had any early morning commitments, so they could afford to have a bit of fun.

Her friends settled on a romantic comedy that had come out the year before, and that Joanna hadn't seen yet, and the three of them relaxed on the couch, the lights dim as they sipped their wine and ate too many brownies.

Halfway through the movie, Ellie got up to feed the dogs dinner. After filling their bowls, she glanced out the kitchen window and saw that the promised snow had come, after all. Large flakes whirled and blew on the other side of the glass, and if she listened, she could hear the moaning of the wind over the laughter of her friends. She shivered and turned away from the window, glad for the company and warmth. She would not want to be outside on a night like this.

Returning to her friends, she sat back down in her spot and pulled an afghan over her legs. "The weather's getting worse," she whispered, so as not to wake Andrew, who had fallen asleep in his play pen. "Both of you can spend the night if you want. There's the bed in the guest room, and the office has a nice daybed that someone else can sleep on."

"Thanks," Joanna whispered back. "I'll call Steve and let him know I'll be home in the morning. What time do they normally get the roads cleared out here?"

"They should be done by eleven at the latest," Ellie responded. "But usually they get the plows out earlier —"

She broke off as the house was suddenly plunged into darkness. None of them made a sound until they heard a loud crashing sound from somewhere over their heads. Ellie jumped, and she heard one of her friends bite back a shriek. A moment later, the lights flickered, and then came back on. The DVD had reset to the menu option, and her phone, sitting on an end table, lit up as the charging cord it was plugged into started supplying power again.

Ellie, Shannon, and Joanna all exchanged wide-eyed looks. Shannon got up to check on her baby while Joanna turned to Ellie.

"What was that noise?" she asked, her voice low.

"I have no idea," Ellie replied. "It sounded like it came from upstairs, didn't it?" She bit her lip, trying to figure out what it could have been. Had some shingles blown off in the storm? She didn't think they would make that loud of a noise. Maybe a limb had fallen off the tree that stood behind the house. She shuddered to think of the damage it might have caused if that was the case.

"He's still sleeping," Shannon said, straightening up from where she was standing by the play pen. "I'm going to go rinse off. I spilled some wine on myself when I jumped after that big crash."

Ellie nodded, trying to calm her pounding heart as she, too, rose. "I'd better go see what that was."

"Let's wait for Shannon to get back," Joanna said. "I'm kind of freaked out, if I'm telling the truth."

She wasn't about to argue with that. She and Joanna waited in the hallway, shifting back and forth and occasionally shooting glances upstairs. Ellie heard the floorboards creak down the hall, but it was only Sawyer, coming out of the kitchen now that he was finished with his meal.

"I bet you didn't even notice that the power went out," she murmured, stroking the lab's head. "You dogs and your obsession with food. The world could end, and you wouldn't notice as long as your muzzle was in a food bowl."

The young dog wagged his tail happily, and Ellie chuckled. It was nice having Sawyer around. Bunny was too small to be much of a protector, though she tried to make up for it with heart. She didn't know if the lab would actually do anything to protect her if a situation ever arose — he had never met a person he didn't like — but at least he *looked* intimidating. That had to count for something.

She heard footsteps and looked up to see Shannon coming out of the hallway that led to the guest bathroom. Her shirt still had spots of wine on it.

"The light in the bathroom isn't working," she explained. "I washed my hands, but I couldn't see well enough from just the hallway light to do my shirt. Do you mind if I throw it in the wash once we're done checking out the noise?"

Ellie was already nodding, even as she frowned. The guest bathroom was the scene of a recent murder, and she hadn't felt comfortable in that room since. Now the lights weren't working, right after a mysterious noise and flickering lights? *I don't believe in ghosts*, she reminded herself.

Clearing her throat, she said, "I'll grab you one of my

t-shirts, and you can wash your shirt. First, though, let's find out what that noise was."

Taking a deep breath, Ellie led the way upstairs with Sawyer at her side and her friends trailing behind her.

CHAPTER FIVE

Whatever Ellie had expected to find, it wasn't nothing. They checked the rooms upstairs, then double checked them. Ellie peered out the windows, wondering if the satellite had somehow been blown off the roof, but saw nothing but more snow.

"*Something* had to have made that noise," she said at last, exasperated. "But nothing's out of place up here."

"Maybe something in the attic?" Joanna suggested.

Ellie frowned. She hadn't been in the attic since they moved in, when she and Russell had brought boxes of miscellanea up. She didn't know what could have made that crashing noise, but it was the last place that they hadn't looked. It was worth a try.

Fetching a flashlight from her bedside table, she rejoined her friends in the hallway and pulled the cord that was attached to the trapdoor. The ladder to the attic unfolded. Biting her lip, Ellie stared up into the darkness, and flicked the flashlight on. She could feel a blast of cold air blowing down at her. *I don't believe in ghosts. I don't.*

"I'll be right back down," she said. "It — it was probably nothing."

She was met with silence. A glance at her friends told her that they were uneasy as well. She turned back to the ladder, wishing she could send Sawyer up ahead of her, but knowing the clumsy dog would never be able to climb the ladder on his own. Taking a deep breath, she began the ascent.

The attic was freezing. That was the first thing that she noticed as she heaved herself up into the dark space. She adjusted the flashlight in her hand and swept the beam around the room. She had barely had a chance to look around when a blast of cold air hit her from behind and she spun around.

The attic window was open. She breathed a sigh of relief. The wind must have done it, somehow. Standing up, she walked over to the window and examined the latch. The wood was splintered, as if something had hit the frame from the other side with great force. Could the wind have done that? She didn't think so.

She felt goosebumps spread across her skin as she spun around, raking the light from the flashlight across the dark room, convinced she was going to see a figure standing in the corner or behind a box, but there was nothing. Nothing but a mess. She wasn't sure how, but the wind must have knocked a couple of boxes over. Two of them had burst open on impact with the ground, spilling papers and clothes across the floor.

"Is everything okay?" Shannon shouted from below.

"It's fine," Ellie called back. "It looks like the wind must have blown the window open up here. The frame is splintered. Can one of you grab me some duct tape? It's in the drawer next to the pantry in the kitchen. I need to fix it well enough that it won't blow open again during the storm."

One of her friends shouted an affirmative, and a couple of minutes later, Joanna appeared, her head and shoulders popping up through the trap doors. She handed the roll of tape to Ellie, then heaved herself up and looked around.

"Wow, did the wind do all of this?"

Ellie handed the flashlight to her friend, then wrestled the window shut and tore off a strip of tape. Russell would probably be able to repair the window frame when he got back, but for now, the duct tape would have to do.

"I guess so," she said as she tore another strip of tape off. "It wasn't this much of a mess before. I haven't even come up here since we brought the boxes up, and I don't think Russell has either."

"I'm glad you've got a guest bed," her friend said, looking around at the snow and scattered items with wide eyes. "If the wind did this to your attic, I don't even want to think about trying to drive home through it."

Ellie tore off one last strip of tape and smoothed it across the frame, then took a step back and eyed her handywork. She didn't know how long the tape would hold, but hopefully it would be good for the rest of the night. Maybe in the morning she could find a wooden board and some nails and could rig up something more solid.

"Let's go finish the movie," she said. "Hopefully all of the excitement is over for the rest of the night."

Ellie woke the next morning to a winter wonderland. The sun was out, and when she looked out her window, the pure, untouched snow that had raged around the house the night before seemed to glitter. The forest behind the house was covered in white, and even the tallest trees seemed to droop under the weight of the snow.

She went downstairs quietly, not wanting to wake her guests. After grabbing Bunny's coat out of the closet, she herded the dogs to the back door. She put the papillon's jacket on, knowing that the little dog would be reluctant to go out in snow that was probably taller than she was, and then opened the door.

She jumped back with a muttered exclamation as snow that had drifted against the house overnight tumbled into the kitchen. Sawyer darted outside, thrilled with the fresh snow to play in. Bunny gave Ellie a disbelieving look and then turned and walked away. Ellie didn't blame her. The snow drifts against the house were higher than her hips. There was no way the pint-sized dog would be able to go out in that.

With a sigh, she trudged back to the front door and pulled on her boots, her winter coat, and her warmest pair of gloves, then grabbed the snow shovel from the front closet.

Clearing even a few square feet around the back door was a challenge. She didn't think she had ever seen so much snow before. Even after she had managed to clear some space, it took some convincing to get Bunny outside. Just as the little dog slunk through the door, Sawyer came running through the snow and clipped Ellie right behind the knees, nearly knocking her over. Yelping, Ellie caught herself with the shovel, then heaved a load of the loose, powdery snow at the big black dog.

"You're going to break my neck one of these days," she said, only half angry as the lab snapped playfully at the shower of snow, then dropped to the ground and rolled in it, turning more white than black.

Laughing, Ellie shook her head. The ominous feeling from the day before was gone, and with the beautiful sight of the new snow and Sawyer's contagious good mood, she was able to nearly forget about all of her worries.

CHAPTER SIX

The snow plows must have started working in the early hours of the morning, because the roads by Ellie's house were cleared by ten. Joanna and Shannon took their leave, both of them eager to get to their own homes and see if they had power. The generator had come on overnight, and Ellie was glad for it. It was one thing to enjoy the beautiful snowfall if she had a nice, toasty house to retreat to; it would be quite another if she had no heat or hot water.

She had already updated the pizzeria's website to let her customers know that the restaurant would be opening a couple of hours later than usual due to the weather, so she had some time on her hands after her friends left. First thing first, she had to let Russell know she had made it through the storm all right. She sat down in front of her computer and began drafting an email to him. She hesitated when she came to the part about the attic window blowing open, and after a moment's thought, she deleted the paragraph about how frightened she had been as she climbed up into the dark attic alone. She didn't want to make him feel bad for leaving. She had told him it was okay, and the last thing she wanted to do was to guilt trip him.

Instead she just told him she had fixed the window as best she could, typed a quick "I love you," and sent the message. Then she leaned back in her chair and drummed her fingers on the table. There really wasn't much else she could do this morning. The generator was still running, which meant the power was still out, and she had to make sure she conserved the fuel. That meant no running the dish-washer or laundry machine. She had already turned the thermostat down a few degrees, and was making sure all of the lights she wasn't currently using were off. With luck, the power would come back on in her area soon, but for now she just had to make sure the generator kept running and was able to keep the house warm enough to keep her and the animals comfortable.

She could head to work early, she supposed, but she had meant to take this extra time off to catch up on some chores. It was beginning to look like she was going to spend the rest of her morning sweeping and mopping. *Mopping...* she thought. Suddenly she remembered the snow that had blown into the attic the night before, and the fact that all of that snow would have melted by now. She hadn't taken the time to see exactly which boxes had been knocked over in the storm, which meant that for all she knew, precious family photos of hers or Russell's could be lying in a puddle of melted snow.

Mentally berating herself for not going up sooner to check on the damage, she shut her laptop, ran into the kitchen to grab some paper towels in case she needed to dry anything, then went upstairs.

The attic was significantly less creepy in the daylight. The single window was hexagonal and large enough to let in plenty of sunlight. There was a single, bare bulb with a dangling chain that she had forgotten about in the rush the night before. The light lit up the corners where the sunlight didn't reach, revealing that most of the boxes were still nicely stacked. The only ones that had been knocked over were those directly in front of the window.

The wind last night must have been stronger than I thought, she thought, frowning. She was still shocked that the storm had managed to blow open the attic window, breaking the wooden frame in the process. *Maybe we have termites*, she thought with a shudder. Termites might have weakened the wood enough for the wind to blow the window open. The house had been inspected before they bought it, but there was no telling what they might have missed.

She began straightening up, lifting the boxes back into their neat stacks and re-packing those items that had fallen out of them. She was glad to find that nothing important had been damaged.

Using the paper towels she had brought up with her, she began mopping up the small puddles of water left behind by the snow. It really wasn't as bad as she had expected. The darkness and the sound of the storm raging outside must have made it seem a lot worse than it really was.

She followed what seemed to almost be a trail of puddles over to an open box near the back of the attic. As she mopped up the last of it, she stood up, glancing down at the large cardboard box the puddles ended at. She really should have done a better job of labeling everything up her, because she couldn't remember what was in it.

Maybe that could be her project for the day; going through the boxes up here and labeling them clearly so she and Russell wouldn't have to go digging through them all whenever they wanted something.

She opened the top of the box and glanced in, expecting to see summer clothes of hers or old case files of Russell's. Instead, the first thing she saw was a vase.

It was a beautiful vase, creamy white with gold accents and stylistic art done around the outside. It was nestled on top of some folded linens. Ellie didn't recognize it, which meant that it was probably her grandmother's. How it had gotten packed in with their stuff, she had no idea. Maybe her grandmother had meant it as a housewarming gift, and had forgotten to mention it, or maybe the older woman had packed it away in a fit of absent mindedness. Regardless of how it had gotten there, it was beautiful. Ellie lifted it, examining it, and on impulse decided to take it downstairs and send some photos to her grandmother to see if she couldn't figure out the history behind it. It had the feel of an antique, and antiques were something Ellie had been getting more and more interested in lately.

Taking one last look around the attic, she tossed the damp paper towels down through the trapdoor, then carefully navigated the ladder with the vase in hand.

CHAPTER SEVEN

E llie got to the pizzeria in plenty of time to prepare for their late opening. The roads in town had long since been cleared, but mountains of snow towered over the cars and pedestrians alike from there the snowplows had deposited it. There were still some people out shoveling sidewalks and parking lots. The pizzeria had a contract with a local snowplow company, so the parking lot had been plowed, but Ellie knew that she would have to spend some time clearing the sidewalk in front of the store.

She didn't think she had ever seen so much snow before. It was simply everywhere. It would be months before it all melted. The snow hills that every parking lot and dead end boasted would survive long into spring. Right now, the fresh snow was beautiful, but as time went by Ellie knew that the pure, white snow would turn grey and dirty as pollution from traffic built up. She was not looking forward to the dreary days of early spring.

The pizzeria wasn't the only business that had gotten a late start. The local schools and the library were both closed for the day, and a fair amount of the small businesses she had passed on her way into town looked dark and empty.

She expected that the pizzeria would easily make up for whatever profits they may have lost by being closed all over, since most of the other small restaurants didn't show any signs of opening. Anyone who didn't have power would be looking for something warm and filling for dinner, and Papa Pacelli's would be the perfect place to go.

By the time Ellie opened the restaurant, the vase she had found had slipped her mind. The condition the attic had been in, however, had not. As she slipped a steaming hot pizza into a box, she found her thoughts drawn back to the night before, when the crash of the window breaking open had coincided almost perfectly with the lights flickering. It hadn't skipped her attention that the one light that had been blown out during the power surge was the bathroom light. The same one where a woman had died not long ago.

Logically, she knew that everything could be explained away as a coincidence. The bathroom light must have been old, it probably would have gone out soon anyway. Same with the wood surrounding the window frame in the attic; termites or a leaky seal could explain why the frame had been weak enough to allow the wind to blow the window open.

But would the wind have been able to knock over the boxes? The more she thought about it, the more her gut told her no. Papers and clothes, which was what most of the boxes held, were pretty heavy when packed into small spaces like that. She could *maybe* see the wind knocking over the box closest to the window, but what about the boxes along the side wall that had fallen? They had been out of the direct path of the wind, and even the strongest gust couldn't change direction like that.

Logically, she didn't believe in ghosts. But somehow logic wasn't all that reassuring at the moment. Ellie was slowly coming to terms with the realization that her house might be haunted, and if the state of the attic was any indication, the resident ghost was very angry.

"Hello? Is anyone here?"

The voice snapped Ellie out of her imagination. She realized she had been standing in the kitchen, staring off into space, when she should have been out front at the register. Someone must have come in while she was zoned out.

"I'm so sorry," she said as she pushed through the door to the front. "It's been a weird day."

The woman at the register looked familiar, but it took Ellie a few moments to match her face to a name. By the time she realized it was Jessie, the woman who had come in with her brothers after her mother's funeral the day before, the other woman was already speaking.

"Oh, that's okay. I was just worried that maybe you weren't open after all. I passed by earlier this morning and your sign was off. I'm half starved, and I really didn't want to eat pizza two days in a row, but nowhere else is open."

"Well, we serve salads too, if you'd rather go with something a bit healthier," Ellie said. "You were staying at a motel, right? I could get you a salad for now, and a small breakfast pizza for tomorrow morning so you don't have to worry about finding somewhere to eat if we get more snow."

"More snow?" Jessie's eyes widened. "Are we supposed to? I'm from a few states further south, and I thought this was a lot of snow."

"We're supposed to be getting snow throughout the week," the pizzeria owner told her. "I know, it seems like it just never lets up, doesn't it?"

"Wow. I hope the roads aren't too bad by the time I have to drive back home. I can't imagine living some-where where it's like this all winter." Jessie shook her head and shot a glance out the window. The sky was still clear, but there were low clouds on the horizon. "What you said sounds good. What's on a breakfast pizza, anyway?"

Ellie smiled. "Whatever you want. Scrambled eggs, sausage, bacon, onions, sweet peppers... and, of course, cheese. You can come up with just about any toppings you'd like, and I'll go get it ready for you. I can add just about anything to your salad too."

"You're a lifesaver," Jessie said. She took a few moments to tell Ellie what she wanted, and Ellie went back into the kitchen to put the orders together and make sure Rose had picked up the next stack of pizzas that were supposed to go out on delivery.

She prepared the Greek salad Jessie had asked for and brought it out along with some ice water and a brownie. "The brownie's on the house," she said as she put the dishes down on the table Jessie had seated herself at. "I remember what you said about why you were here yesterday, and I hope things are looking up for you."

"Thanks." Jessie gave her a small smile and reached for the water. After taking a sip, she said, "I wish I could say things were getting better, but honestly, everything's worse. One of my brothers is fighting the will, the other brother isn't speaking to him, and neither of them are very happy with me at the moment either. It looks like I'm going to have to be here for a while."

"I'm sorry." Ellie hesitated. "Do you want to talk about any of it? I know I'm a stranger, but sometimes it helps to bounce ideas off of someone who isn't involved."

The other woman shook her head. "Thanks, but I kind of want to just forget about it all for now. Besides, you probably wouldn't believe me if I told you half the crazy stuff that was going on in my life."

"I don't know, I'm starting to have a pretty open mind." Ellie chuckled. "I'm slowly coming to the conclusion that my house is haunted. I doubt anything you could tell me would be weirder than that."

"Oh, really?" Jessie's eyes widened. "I *love* haunted

houses. I was on an amateur paranormal investigation team for a while back in college. We never found any solid evidence that could prove ghosts were real, but I definitely felt something a few times. Do you want me to come look around?"

Ellie blinked. Her reflex was to say no, but after everything that had happened in her house, she was beginning to realize she had to be more open to the possibility that there was more out there than she wanted to believe.

"You know what? Sure. If any house is haunted, mine is." She hesitated, then lowered her voice. "More than one person has been killed there. I'm not usually superstitious, but something just feels off about the place."

Jessie's eyes shone with excitement. "Tell me when you get off work, and I'll come over."

CHAPTER EIGHT

Jessie returned to the pizzeria just as Ellie was locking the front doors. She smiled and waved, then rolled down the driver's side window and handed Ellie a coffee.

"I stopped at the cafe on the corner and thought you might want something too. I didn't know what you liked, so I just got you a vanilla latte. I hope that's okay."

"It's perfect," Ellie said. "Thanks. I just finished up here. Do you want to follow me back to my house?"

The other woman nodded. "Lead the way."

Ellie took her time driving back home, making sure Jessie could easily keep up with her. Ever since agreeing to this, she had been having doubts. Was it really smart to invite a stranger over to her home while she was there alone? What did she hope to gain from this? Even though she was spooked by the eerie events of the night before, she wasn't fully convinced that ghosts were real. She wasn't sure what to expect from Jessie's visit, and knew that she would take anything the other woman said with a grain of salt.

She pulled into her driveway and shut off her engine. Jessie pulled in behind her and joined her on the front stoop.

"I have dogs," Ellie warned belatedly as she pushed the front door open. "They're both friendly, but the lab is young and still tries to jump up on people sometimes. Just ignore him until he calms down. If he gets too rambunctious, push him away."

Sawyer and Bunny greeted her excitedly, then turned their attention to her guest, who stepped into the house and shut the door behind her. She followed Ellie's advice and ignored Sawyer, who was bouncing up and down in front of her, and took off her coat, handing it to her host.

"Should I take my shoes off?"

"Whatever you're more comfortable with. If you're going up in the attic, you might want to leave them on so you don't have to worry about getting a splinter. The floor boards up there aren't great."

Jessie nodded and left her shoes on, bending down to let Bunny sniff her hand and to give Sawyer, who had calmed down enough to sit still at her feet, a scratch behind the ears.

"It's a small world," she said as she straightened up. She looked around with a smile on her face. "When we turned onto this road, something told me you were going to pull into this driveway. I can't believe you live here, it's such a coincidence."

"What are you talking about?" Ellie asked with a frown.

"My parents best friends used to live in this house. My brothers and I were here all the time when we were kids. You've changed some stuff, but I still recognize it. I actually really like what you've done with the place. If I remember correctly, the walls used to be covered with the ugliest wallpaper in the world. It looks so much better now."

The pizzeria owner blinked, too stunned to respond right away. It *was* a coincidence, and a pretty major one. Sure, Kittiport was a small town, but it wasn't *that* small. At last, she said, "Did you set this up or something? Is that what you and your brothers do, convince people their houses are haunted and then prey on them when they're convinced they're going crazy?"

"No, no." Jessie raised her hands, looking hurt. "Seriously, I had no idea you lived here until just now. It *is* a coincidence, I promise. I'm not charging money or anything, so where would the benefit in something like that be for me? Like I said, I'm interested in the paranormal, but it's just a hobby. I haven't actually been involved in the community for years. And my brothers both think I'm a bit crazy as it is, they've never been interested in the same stuff I am. I swear, this is just a weird coincidence. It makes me think that there might really be something going on here. Oh, I wish I'd brought my recording equipment."

Frowning, Ellie shifted on her feet, considering what the other woman had said. "All right," she said at last. "Let's head upstairs. You can take a look at the attic. If you want to look at the guest bathroom too, go ahead. That's where... where the person died."

Jessie nodded, then gestured for Ellie to lead the way.

At first, the pizzeria owner watched curiously as Jessie walked slowly around the room, but after a while she got bored and went downstairs to take care of the animals. She still wasn't completely comfortable with the other woman being there, but Jessie seemed harmless enough if a bit eccentric.

By the time she came downstairs, the dogs had eaten dinner and Marlowe was working her way through a bowl of fresh fruit. "I'm ready to see the guest bathroom now," Jessie said.

"It's through here." Ellie led her down the hall. "Sorry, the light is still out. I haven't replaced it yet. I'll go grab bulbs now."

When she returned with the new light bulbs, she found Jessie staring into the mirror. Ellie cleared her throat, and the other woman jumped slightly.

"Sorry," she said. "I'll get out of your way so you can change out the bulbs if you want."

"Did you... sense... anything?" the pizzeria owner asked as she began unscrewing the burnt-out bulbs.

"I'm not sure," Jessie said. "I thought I smelled a cologne or perfume up there that seemed familiar, but it could have been something that you or your husband wears. And down here in the bathroom... well, I'm not sure if it's my mind playing tricks on me because I know someone died in here, but it does seem a bit colder than the rest of the house, doesn't it? And there's that stain on the ceiling. It could be water damage, or it could be an impression left by a spirit." She sighed. "I really wish I was still in touch with the people who were in the paranormal club at college. I was hoping there would be something obvious, something that screamed *yes, there is a ghost here*, but I should have known better. There never is."

Ellie nodded. She hadn't really expected Jessie to find any solid evidence of paranormal activity. "I'll keep on being a skeptic, then," she said, giving the other woman a smile. "Thanks for coming over. At the very least, it was a reminder that I needed to replace these bulbs." She stepped back and flicked on the light switch. The lights came on, then with a quiet popping sound, the bulbs went dark.

CHAPTER NINE

J essie stayed for another half-an-hour after the light bulbs went dead. She spent most of that time in the guest bathroom, trying different things to get the ghost to "show itself" again. Ellie wasn't sure what the other woman was expecting, but whatever it was, it seemed that it didn't happen. She left disappointed, but hopeful that something interesting might happen in the future. If it did, Ellie was supposed to call her immediately.

The pizzeria owner felt a bit baffled after the other woman was gone. She wasn't sure where she stood on the whole ghost issue after all of this. On one hand, a lot had happened in the house recently that wasn't easy for her to explain away. On the other hand, all of it *could* be explained away if she let her imagination run wild, and she hadn't actually seen anything that convinced her there was a ghost. Sometimes coincidences were just coincidences, not the restless dead.

She decided to do what she could to put the whole issue out of her mind. It was late, but she had another couple of hours before she needed to be in bed. The wind outside had begun to pick up again, to the point where she couldn't tell if it was snowing or if the snow in the air was just being picked up and blown by the gusts. Thankfully the power was back on and the generator was quiet. The house was warm and comfortable, and she had a delicious pizza waiting for her for dinner. It was the perfect evening to get comfortable on the couch and turn on a movie.

Ellie woke hours later with a crick in her neck and the sound of the DVD's menu playing on repeat. Somehow, she had managed to fall asleep on the couch, and she was already regretting it. A warm weight on her legs told her that Sawyer had climbed up to join her, and Bunny was curled up on a blanket that had fallen to the floor. The house creaked over her head, and she felt goosebumps rise on her skin. She had to remind herself that it was just the wind.

"Get off my legs, Sawyer," she muttered, kicking her feet. One of her legs had fallen asleep, thanks to the big black dog's weight. The lab slipped off the couch and onto the floor stretching for a long moment before trotting over to the door with a whine.

"Yeah, I'll put you outside before we go up to bed." Ellie covered up a yawn. "Just give me a second to wake up. I'm too old to be sleeping on couches."

She got to her feet, wiggling her toes as the sensation of pins and needles flooded the leg that had been asleep. When Sawyer suddenly let out a booming bark, she was so surprised that she nearly fell over. She turned to look at him just as the big lab ran to the window in the living room and put his feet up on the windowsill, looking outside.

Ellie was glad that the only light in the room was from the TV. She grabbed the remote and flicked the screen off as Sawyer continued to bark, then joined him at the window, pushing the curtains aside so she could look out.

At first, she didn't see anything, but then through the blowing snow she saw a humanoid figure moving across the front lawn. It disappeared as quickly as she had seen it, leaving her to wonder if it had really been there. Sawyer certainly seemed to think so.

Her heart pounding, she grabbed the lab by the collar and dragged him away from the window. Keeping him close beside her, she made her way through the house, checking to make sure the doors were locked and turning off the lights so whoever was outside wouldn't be able to see in easily.

Why did Russell have to choose this *week to be gone?* she thought. A rush of adrenaline had hit her when she had first seen the figure outside, and now her palms prickled as she pulled the curtains in the office closed. She didn't know what to do next. Should she call the police? Would they take her seriously if she called complaining about a figure walking through the yard at night? Did she even have something to worry about? True, it wasn't exactly normal for someone to be taking a walk during a snowstorm in the middle of the night, but it *could* be one of her neighbors out on a late night walk with their dog.

A loud thump jolted her out of her thoughts. Sawyer started barking again, and took off running toward the kitchen. Ellie went from trying to rationalize everything that had happened to a blind panic. She followed the dog into the kitchen and grabbed the biggest knife out of the knife block. Sawyer was barking at the back door this time.

There was another thump, then silence. Feeling as though her heart was about to burst, Ellie carefully peeked out of the kitchen window. She saw nothing but white outside.

Russell, she thought. *I need to call Russell.* Dragging Sawyer with her, she retreated to the living room to grab her cell phone. She dialed her husband's number, but he didn't answer. A glance at the clock told her he was probably long since asleep. Torn between her fear, and the knowledge that if she called the police and it was nothing, she would never hear the end of it, she decided to settle in for a long night of watchfulness. Here in the living room, with the dogs, her cell phone, and the kitchen knife, she should be safe enough. She made a silent promise to herself to call the police if anything else happened.

By the time the sun rose, she was passed out on the couch with the dogs on the floor and the knife forgotten on the coffee table.

CHAPTER TEN

S awyer's barking woke her in the morning. She was disoriented at first, but memories of the night before came quickly flooding back. She sat bolt upright on the couch, ignoring the stiffness of her neck, and looked around. The light coming in through the curtains told her it was morning, and her phone confirmed the time. It was shortly after eight. She had made it through the night, no worse for the wear. *It's good I didn't call the police*, she thought. *They would have come out here for nothing.*

Sawyer was at the window, staring out through the glass as he carried on. Ellie got up and moved to pull him away. Her hand fell short when she saw what had caught his attention. Parked across the road were a handful of emergency vehicles. She recognized one of the deputies cruisers and the vehicle from the local morgue. Something sour turned over in her stomach.

She hurried to the front door, where she pulled on her boots. She was wrestling with her coat when someone knocked on the front door. Nudging Sawyer and Bunny out of the way with her legs, she pulled the door open to find Bethany's familiar face frowning at her.

"Hi, Ms. Ward. Were you on your way out?"

Ellie glanced down at her outerwear, then shook her head. "I was just going to see what's going on across the street."

"I see. That's good, I need to ask you a few questions anyway and I'd hate to make you late for work. Would you rather talk inside or out here?"

"We can talk inside, if you don't mind the dogs."

She stepped aside and Bethany came in. She had a grim look on her face, but agreed to go into the kitchen with Ellie. Ellie gestured to the stools at the island for Bethany to take a seat, then turned on the coffee maker before joining her.

"So, what happened?" she asked, bracing herself for the worst.

"Someone spotted a body by the side of the road while they were driving to work," Bethany said. "The man looks like he's been dead for some time. Blunt force trauma to the head. We're still working out just what happened and trying to ID him. It's right across from your house. Is there any chance you heard or saw something last night?"

Guilt rushed through Ellie. "Yes," she said. "I... I knew I should have called the police. Around midnight, Sawyer started barking at something outside. I looked out the window and thought I saw someone walking through the yard, but I wasn't a hundred percent sure, not with the snow and wind. I went around the house and made sure all the doors were locked and the lights were off. A few minutes later, I heard two thumps around by the back of the house. I looked outside but couldn't see anything. Nothing else happened, and I fell asleep a couple of hours later. I actually just woke up a few minutes ago when Sawyer started barking out the window at the emergency vehicles."

Bethany took a couple of moments to make notes on her notepad. At last, she looked up. "Did you hear anything else? Did the person say anything? Did you see or hear anything to indicate that there might have been more than one person?"

The pizzeria owner shook her head. "No to all of that. I don't think I would have been able to hear anything over the wind even if whoever it was did say something."

Bethany sighed and ran her hand through her hair. "And I take it you have no idea why someone would be wandering around outside your house during a snowstorm? Have you or Russell gotten any threats recently?"

"Not that I know of," she said. "I'm sure he'd tell me if someone had threatened him. There's no way he would have gone to the conference if he thought there was a reason to worry."

"I figured." Bethany put her notebook away. "I hate it when we get cases like this when Russell isn't around. No ID on him, blunt force trauma that doesn't match trauma we'd expect to see from an impact with a car, no murder weapon that we can find, and of course the snow is hiding goodness knows what. We're searching the area now, but the storm isn't doing us any favors. I hate to ask it of you, but could you come see if you can ID the body before we take him away? If you recognize him, it will save us a lot of work."

"I'll come," Ellie said, even though the last thing she wanted was to take a look at a corpse. Her stomach twisted as she crossed her fingers, hoping it *wasn't* anyone she knew.

She wasn't that lucky. Outside, the cold wind whipping crystals of snow into her eyes, she stared unblinkingly at the dead man's face. She knew him, but not well. It was one of Jessie's brothers, the younger one who she recognized as a regular at the pizzeria. Iggy.

CHAPTER ELEVEN

The first thing Ellie did when Bethany left was to call Russell. He had returned her call from the night before while she was sleeping, and she hadn't had a chance to get back in touch with him during the chaos of the morning. She had a lot to tell him.

"I'm glad you called back," he said when he answered the phone. "I was getting worried. I saw that you called me in the middle of the night last night. Is everything okay?"

She hated that the answer was no. Taking a deep breath, she told him all about what had happened the night before, which led to her telling him about Jessie, which in turn meant that she had to back-track all the way to the attic window being blown open and the lights in the guest bathroom going out.

"All of this happened in just the past few days?" She could imagine him running a hand through his short hair or rubbing at his temples. "I'm coming back, Ellie."

"No, Russell... I don't want you to have to cut your trip short." Ellie bit her lip. She *wanted* him to come back, but she also wanted him to enjoy himself. "I know it sounds like a lot, but it's probably just a lot of weird coincidences."

"Ellie..."

"Look, I'll admit that I've been spooked pretty much all week. This is all freaking me out. But if you come running back every single time I find myself in some sort of trouble... well, let's just say I don't exactly lead a boring life. You'll never be able to go anywhere. It's not fair that I get to travel down to Florida a couple of times a year without a care in the world, but you can't so much as go to a business conference without having things break down here."

"There's a possible murder case, Ellie. A body was found in front of our house. I'm needed there."

"Would you really be coming back because of that, or because you're worried about me?" His silence told her all that she needed to know. "Just... don't make a snap decision about it. At least catch the conference today. If anything else happens or you still feel like you need to come back, just grab an early flight tomorrow and I'll pick you up before work."

"Fine," he said. "But you have to promise to call me the second something else happens."

"I will," she said. "I love you."

"I love you too."

She said her goodbyes then hung up, feeling a bit bad as she did so. Had she been too harsh? She missed Russell horribly, which was one of the reasons she *didn't* want him to come back. Both of them were successful, independent adults with careers that they loved. She didn't want to stand in Russell's way just because she was feeling lonely and jumpy in the empty house. Sometimes she still felt like she was new to the whole being married thing, and seemed to constantly second guess herself. While logically she knew that Russell loved her, there was still a part of her that had been wounded by the way her previous relationship had ended and was desperate not to be a burden to her new husband. She wanted to prove that she could still handle things on her own. She just wasn't sure whether she was trying to prove that to Russell, or herself.

The morning had been non-stop chaos from the moment she had woken up, and she was still sore from sleeping so awkwardly on the couch, so she took a much needed hot shower before making herself some oatmeal and a scrambled egg for breakfast. She had downed a cup of coffee on an empty stomach while Bethany was there, and it had left her feeling jittery. It felt good to get some warm food in her stomach.

She finished getting ready for the day, then turned her attention to the rest of the house. She had gotten behind on the basic housekeeping with all of the chaos of the past few days, and decided to spend some time getting things tidied up. That way, if Russell *did* come home early, the house would be ready for him.

Humming to herself, she walked into the office armed with a broom and dustpan. Since the office was where they put the dogs when she needed them to be out of the way, it was a prime spot for dust bunnies — or rather, dog fur bunnies. She pulled open the curtains and started sweeping the floor,

PATTI BENNING

only stopping when her eyes landed on the gorgeous vase that she had completely forgotten about. Deciding she had better email her grandmother about it before she forgot again, she carried it into the kitchen where the lighting was better and took some photos of it with her cell phone. She attached them to an email and sent it, then put the vase by the sink as a reminder to herself to wash it later.

She got back to work, feeling good about having the house clean. At the very least, she would be coming home to a clean house this evening, and that was worth the work now.

CHAPTER TWELVE

A few hours later, Ellie was in the middle of making a fresh batch of pesto sauce at the pizzeria when Iris poked her head into the kitchen and said, "There's someone out here who wants to see you."

Ellie put the basil leaves down and went to the sink to wash her hands. "Can you finish this up? And do you have any idea who it is?"

"I have no idea," Iris said. "It's a guy, maybe about your age, with dark hair. He didn't say what he wanted."

"Next time, can you make sure to ask what they want? Sometimes it's something you or another employee could help them with. I don't mind it if I'm not in the middle of anything, but when I'm busy and have to stop what I'm doing just to help someone with something like recovering a lost gift card or answering questions about allergies, it can be kind of distracting."

"Sorry," her employee said. "I can go back out and ask of you want."

"Don't worry about it right now, I'll go see what's up. Just keep it in mind for later. A lot of people seem to think that only the boss can handle certain things, when really you guys are perfectly capable of handling just about anything." Ellie smiled at the younger woman. "Really, you or Jacob or Rose could probably run this place. In a couple of months, Pete could too. I couldn't ask for better employees."

Iris grinned. "Thanks, Ms. P."

After wiping her hands dry on a towel, Ellie stepped out into the front area of the pizzeria. The man standing on the other side of the counter looked hauntingly familiar. She may not have recognized him if she hadn't seen his brother's body just hours before.

"You're Jessie's brother, right?" she asked as she approached him.

He nodded and held out his hand. "Marcus, but everyone calls me Mark."

"It's nice to meet you," she said, shaking his hand. She was about to give her condolences about his brother's death, but bit her tongue. Did he know yet? She wasn't sure how quickly the police would have contacted him, and she didn't want him to hear it from her first.

It turned out that she didn't have to worry about it. "I heard you were the one who found Iggy."

"I didn't find him," she said. "That was someone else. But he was right across the street from my house, and I'm the one who identified him."

He nodded, his jaw clenching. "Can I talk to you in private?"

"Sure, um, is this corner booth okay?" There were only two other people in the pizzeria, both of them on the other side of the room.

"It'll do."

She led the way over, then nervously asked if she could get him a drink. He declined, and she took a seat across from him. She wasn't sure what he'd want to know, but she knew that whatever it was, it was bound to be painful.

"It came to my attention that my sister was at your house yesterday," he began. Ellie blinked. This wasn't what she was expecting at all. "She met with Iggy and me last night, and started going on about ghosts in the Potters' house. Now, I won't judge you on your beliefs, but I think you should know that Jessie isn't the most trustworthy person when it comes to that sort of thing. She's been crying wolf for as long as I can remember, always convinced she saw a ghost or a spirit. Iggy always got dragged into it, and you can see how well that ended for him."

The Potters, she thought. They must have been the family friends Jessie had mentioned had used to live in her house. "I'm sorry, I don't see what you're getting at," she said, frowning. "I'm so sorry for your brother's death, but I wasn't aware it had anything to do with my home."

As she said it, she began to feel stupid. Of *course* it had something to do with her. Her terrible luck aside, what were the chances that Iggy would have decided to go for a walk by her house in the middle of the night during a snowstorm the same day his sister had come over for an impromptu ghost hunting session? The fact that she hadn't connected the two things before only made her realize how frazzled she was.

"I don't know the details, but my guess is Jessie dragged Iggy out to your house with stories of ghosts. Things have been... strained between the three of us since our mother's death. She was rather well off, and Jessie feels that her possessions were divided unfairly in the will. Iggy inherited something of great value from her, and with Jessie's money problems, well, I'm not surprised things ended up how they did. I don't think she has any reason to hurt you, but if you hear from her again, can you contact me immediately? Here's my business card."

He handed her a card. Ellie took it and placed it on

the table, staring at it for a moment as she gathered her thoughts. "Are you saying you think Jessie killed your brother?" she asked, her eyes widening as his words sank in.

"I don't have any proof, but it's the only thing that makes sense." Mark sighed and leaned back, rubbing his eyes with one hand. For the first time, Ellie noticed how tired he looked. *It's no wonder,* she thought. *He lost his mother and his brother in such a short span of time, and he believes his sister was responsible for one of the deaths.* "I have no idea where Jessie's staying. She probably paid in cash, so there's no way to track her down, and she hasn't been answering her phone. Just be careful. I don't want her to hurt anyone else."

Ellie stared at him, not sure what to say. Jessie a killer? It didn't fit with what she knew of the other woman, but really, what did she know about her? What did she know about Mark, for that matter? Could she trust him?

"I'll be careful," she promised at last. "And I'll let you know if I see her again."

He nodded once. "Thanks. I'll get out of your hair now. You seem like a good woman, and I'm sorry my sibling involved you in all of this."

CHAPTER THIRTEEN

E llie drove home late that evening with her mind full of thoughts about Jessie and her siblings. She knew that Russell would want to know what Mark had said, and she was already mentally drafting their conversation. She didn't think she had it in her to argue against his coming home early again. The simple truth was, it would be nice to have him there. This was all getting to be a bit too much for her to want to handle on her own.

She parked her car in the driveway and walked up to the front door, fiddling with the keys until she found the right one. She slid it into the deadbolt and turned it, then frowned. The deadbolt was already undone. *I probably just forgot to lock it on my way out the door this morning*, she told herself. She felt goose-bumps rise on her skin. No, she *knew* she had locked it. She was always careful about locking up behind her — living with the sheriff would do that to anyone — and had been doubly careful about it the past few days.

If it hadn't been for the fact that she could hear the dogs on the other side of the door — punctuated by a call from Marlowe; the bird knew from the commotion the dogs were making that she was home — she probably would have turned around and gotten right back in her car to call Bethany. Instead, worried about the animals, she pushed the door open. Sawyer and Bunny mobbed her just inside the door. She crouched down to pet them, making sure that both of them were unhurt. If someone had broken in, at least they hadn't done anything to the dogs.

She stood up, still feeling uncomfortable. How could someone have gotten in the house with the doors and windows all locked? The only other people with a key in town were Shannon and James, and neither of them would have stopped by without telling her about it. For that matter, who would have broken in with Sawyer barking like mad? He wouldn't hurt a fly, but most people wouldn't know that —

Ellie's train of thought broke off as the obvious answer occurred to her. Jessie. The other woman had visited the day before and knew that the dogs were friendly. That wouldn't explain how she had unlocked the deadbolt from outside, and it was still just a guess that someone had even been in the house at all, but Ellie was *certain* that the door had been locked when she left.

"Let's go check the house, guys," she said to the dogs. "Then I'll put you out and get you dinner." At the word 'dinner,' their ears perked up.

She searched the bottom floor of the house for any sign that someone had forced entry, but found nothing obvious. There were a few things here and there that seemed out of place, but she didn't know if it was just her mind playing tricks on her. She had almost convinced herself that the entire thing was all in her head and she had forgotten to lock the front door that morning when, walking past the bottom of the stairs, she felt a draft.

A sharp whistle called Sawyer's attention back to her, and she went upstairs with the big dog at her heels. Even before she saw it, something told her what she would find. The trapdoor to the attic was open, the ladder down, and a cold breeze was coming in from above.

Ellie had been on edge a lot over the past few days, but nothing could compare to the chill she felt in her veins at the sight of the open attic door. The sudden certainty that someone had been in her house, *might still be in her house*, stole her breath away. She stood frozen in place for long seconds before a nudge from Sawyer jolted her into action. She ran downstairs and grabbed her phone, dialing the number for the police with shaking hands.

"I checked every nook and cranny, and no one's here," Bethany said an hour later. Ellie, who had been waiting nervously in the kitchen, felt herself relax fractionally.

"Thank goodness," she breathed. "What happens next?"

"I'll make sure you've got an officer keeping watch for the rest of the night. If you can think of anyone who might have had motive to break in, give me their name and any information you have."

"I do know someone who might have done it." She told the deputy what she knew about Jessie. "But how did she even get in in the first place?"

"It looks like she came in through the attic window, oddly enough. The tree behind your house is perfect for climbing, and there is a trail in the snow on the roof leading from the largest limb over to the attic window. Do you have any idea why she might have broken in?"

"She's obsessed with the paranormal, and she thinks my house might be haunted," Ellie said. At Bethany's disbelieving look, she shrugged. "I honestly don't have the slightest idea other than that."

"Well, if you think of anything, let me know. Do you have someone who can stay with you tonight?"

"I'll call my friend Joanna," Ellie told her. "She'd probably be willing to come over. And I'm sure Russell will come home tomorrow. I'm going to end up giving the poor guy a heart attack one of these days."

"That would be a shame, it would be a pain to find a new sheriff." Bethany smiled to show that she was joking, then gave Ellie a serious look. "Are you sure you're okay with me leaving now? Do you want me to wait until your friend gets here?"

"I'll be fine," the pizzeria owner promised. "I'm going to call Joanna, then I'm going to call Russell. By the time I get off the phone with him, Joanna will probably be here. And so will the officer who will be watching the house tonight, right?"

The deputy nodded. "If you have any trouble, all you'll have to do is shout."

"I can manage that," Ellie said. "Thanks for getting out here so quickly. I wish the person who broke in had still been here, so all of this could just be over."

Bethany gave her a strange look. "You really wish you'd been alone in the house with this person?"

Ellie shivered. "On second thought, maybe not."

CHAPTER FOURTEEN

Ellie's prediction had been wrong; she was still talking to Russell by the time Joanna pulled into the driveway. She opened the front door for her friend, waved to the officer across the street to let him know it was all right, then made an apologetic face at Joanna as the other woman came inside.

"I should get going," she said into the phone. "Joanna just got here."

"All right, if you're absolutely sure you're safe. Are you sure you don't want me to come on the earlier flight tomorrow?"

"I really can't take the time off of work," she said. "The flight won't get in until noon, and I'm supposed to be working in the morning. The schedule has been crazy enough this week as it is. It's not fair of me to switch the shifts around last minute all the time and expect my employees to be able to cover them, just because I'm the boss. I'll be able to pick you up tomorrow evening. That will give you the day to catch more of the conference."

"What if whoever broke in comes back while you're at work?"

"Joanna said she'll stay here during the day, and the police are going to be doing drive-bys every hour. Bethany told me that this is a high-priority case, due to the man who passed away here last night."

"I wish I could find an earlier flight." He sighed. "All right, I'll see you tomorrow evening. Let me know if anything else happens, okay?"

"I will," she promised. "I'm sorry you have to come home early from the conference."

"It's not your fault at all. Don't feel bad, okay? Just take care of yourself. And tell Joanna to be careful too. I don't want anyone getting hurt."

"We'll be fine," she promised.

They said their goodbyes and she ended the call, turning to her friend with an apologetic smile on her face. "I didn't mean for that to take so long. He's got to fly back in to Portland, and he needs me to pick him up. Neither of the available flights was at a great time."

"Don't worry about it," Joanna said. "From what you told me, you've had a crazy day. You've gotta fill me in. What exactly has been going on since our girls' night in?"

Ellie led the way into the kitchen to pour them each a glass of wine as she began telling Joanna the story.

The night passed without further incident. Ellie spotted a police cruiser driving by the house twice as she got ready for work, so it seemed like Bethany had been right when she had promised Ellie the house would be watched throughout the day. She still felt bad leaving Joanna there alone, but her friend didn't seem to mind.

"It's like a mini-vacation," she said as she said goodbye to the pizzeria owner. "There's pizza in the fridge, movies by the TV, and a couple of cute pooches to hang out with. I'll be living it up while you're slaving away over the stove all day."

"You have the number for the police, right? If you see anyone suspicious, anyone at all, don't hesitate to call. Remember, the break-in could be related to the murder, so don't take any chances."

"I'll be fine," her friend promised. "Go to work. You're going to be late."

Ellie glanced at the time and winced. Joanna was right, she was cutting it close. With one last wave goodbye, she turned and walked over to her car. Only a few more hours until her husband was back in town. She had no doubts that Russell would get to the bottom of the mystery quickly, and things would then go back to normal.

She almost wasn't surprised when she got the call from Joanna a few hours later. Even before picking up the phone, something told her that her friend was calling with bad news.

"Hey, Ellie," Joanna said when she answered. "I don't want you to freak out, but someone just broke a kitchen window. The police are here and no one's hurt, but whoever did it got away."

Ellie groaned and leaned her forehead against the stainless-steel fridge. "Give me half an hour and I'll head over," she said. "Whoever's behind all of this is determined to get inside, and I want to be there if they try again."

CHAPTER FIFTEEN

By the time Ellie got home, the police had gone. Joanna was sweeping up the broken glass when she walked into the kitchen.

"Here, let me do that," the pizzeria owner said. "Tell me what happened."

"I was in the living room on my laptop when I heard the sound of breaking glass and the dogs started freaking out. I ran into the kitchen to see someone reaching through the window, trying to unlock the door. When they saw me, they took off running. I called the police, and you know the rest."

"Did you get a good look at the person?"

Joanna shook her head. "Whoever it was was wearing a ski mask. It all happened so fast, and I was freaking out. I know you warned me they might come back, but I didn't think something like this would actually happen."

Ellie dumped the broken glass in the garbage can, then took some damp paper towels and ran them across the floor to pick up the smaller shards she might have missed. "I'm glad you're okay. I'm going to stick around here until it's time for me to go pick Russell up this evening. You can head home if you want. I'm sure today has been more than you bargained for."

"I'll stay," Joanna said. "Clara's running the hot dog shop and Steve's at work, so I don't have anything to do anyway, and I don't want to leave you here on your own. What on earth did you get yourself into this time?"

"I have no idea," Ellie said with a sigh.

Once the glass was cleaned up, Ellie made her way to the office, where Joanna had put the dogs so they wouldn't get their feet cut on the glass or get in the way of the police. She checked their paws over to make sure they hadn't gotten hurt, then patted them both on the head.

"I guess you aren't that much of a deterrent after all, Sawyer. This is one determined robber."

She sat down at the desk to call Russell and give him an update. As she did so, her elbow bumped the mouse and her computer's screen came to life. She noticed a notification for an unread email message and clicked to open the program. It was a message from her grandmother. She had all but forgotten the email she had sent about the vase. Her breath caught as she read the response.

I don't recognize that vase. Maybe it's something of Russell's? It looks quite expensive, whatever it is. I showed the photos to my friend, Angela, and she thinks it could be a valuable antique.

How is everything there? I miss you, but I can't say I miss the snow. I heard about the storms you've been having up there. I hope you're pulling through. How are the tenants in my house doing? When are you coming to visit?

Give my love to Russell.

From,

Nonna

She didn't know why it had taken her so long to

make the connection. Her grandmother's message was the missing link. Suddenly, everything made more sense than it had since the night of the storm.

The attic window hadn't blown open. Someone had broken in. The trail of melted snow leading to the box where she had found the vase hadn't been a strange coincidence, it had been a melted trail of footprints. Someone had broken in that night, not to steal something, but to leave something behind. The vase wasn't hers or her grandmother's or even Russell's; it belonged to whoever kept trying to break back in to her house. The vase was the reason the attic had been ransacked, and it was the reason someone had broken the kitchen window today. It was sitting in plain view on the counter next to the sink.

Mark's words came back to her. His mother had left something very valuable to Iggy in her will, something that Jessie wanted. That something could only be the vase. Why it had been hidden in her attic, Ellie had no idea, but she finally felt as though she was on the right track. With just a few more answers, she might actually be able to solve this mystery once and for all.

CHAPTER SIXTEEN

With a tingle of excitement, Ellie went to the kitchen and retrieved the vase, bringing it with her into the office where she set it on the desk next to the computer. It took her longer than she had expected to find information about it, but at last she found a matching vase online. When she saw what it was worth, she gasped. The vase had a value of nearly twenty thousand dollars. It had been last sold at an auction thirty years ago, and had a twin that was currently on display at a museum in Washington.

Ellie stared at the vase, mentally replaying every time she had recklessly lifted it or set it down somewhere. It was pure luck that it hadn't fallen and shattered, especially with the dogs in the house.

I need to figure out who it actually belongs to, she thought. *If this is what Mark was talking about — and it has to be — then it was rightfully Iggy's. Now that he's gone, whose is it?* She decided that her best course of action would be to let Russell handle it. It very well could be important in Iggy's murder case.

Before she could pick up the phone to call her husband, someone knocked on the front door. Ellie put the vase on a high shelf in the office, carefully out of reach of the dogs, then went to answer the door.

Joanna had beat her to it. When Ellie saw her friend chatting with Jessie, she froze. Mark's warnings about his sister came rushing back. Looking at Jessie, it was hard to imagine that she'd had anything to do with Iggy's death. She looked open and friendly, if a little tired.

"Hey," she said when she saw Ellie. "I was just telling your friend, I'm looking for something. This is probably going to sound strange, but I think my brother hid something in your house. Do you mind if I come in and take a look around?"

Joanna shot Ellie a puzzled glance. The pizzeria owner moved forward to stand next to her friend. Alarm bells were going off in her head. This couldn't be a coincidence. Jessie had to be talking about the vase, the same vase a robber had just failed to steal from the kitchen counter. *She tried to steal it just hours ago, and now she's trying a different way to get it*, Ellie thought.

"I'm sorry, but I've had a lot of crazy stuff going on these past few days," she said. "I'm not comfortable letting someone I don't know well in."

"Oh." The other woman's face fell. "Okay. I understand."

"What do you mean, your brother hid something here?" Joanna asked, frowning at Jessie. Ellie bit back a groan. She hadn't had a chance to tell her friend about her discovery yet. She still wasn't sure why someone had hidden the vase in her house in the first place, and she was more concerned with keeping it and both of them safe than finding out what exactly was going on.

"It's a long story," Jessie said. "I could come in and tell it, I guess —"

"No." Ellie knew she sounded harsh, but she didn't like this situation at all. "I'm sorry, but I'm not comfortable with this."

Jessie looked hurt. "I understand. If you change your mind, will you give me a call? My cell phone's broken, but you can call room six at the Marigold Motel if you want to get in touch with me."

"Okay," the pizzeria owner said. "And... I'm sorry about your brother. This can't have been an easy week for you, either."

"Thanks. He didn't deserve what happened to him. It's all my mom's fault. That stupid will..." She shook her head. "I'll get out of your hair."

They traded stiff goodbyes. Ellie waited until she saw Jessie pull away, then she shut and locked the door.

"What was that all about?" Joanna asked.

"Come with me. I've got something to show you."

CHAPTER SEVENTEEN

Joanna was just as shocked as Ellie had been to learn the value of the vase. "I just don't understand why someone would hide it in the attic," she said. "That lady said her brother hid it, didn't she? It doesn't make any sense."

"I don't know why either, but I know someone who might be able to tell us," Ellie said. "I'll be right back, I need to go get my wallet."

She returned a moment later with her wallet and Mark's business card clutched in her hand "What are you doing?" her friend asked.

"Her brother asked me to call him if I saw her again. I'm going to see if he can shed some light on what's going on."

She dialed the number and put her cell phone on speaker mode. Mark answered after a couple of rings. "It's Eleanora Ward, from Papa Pacelli's," she said when he answered. "I just spoke to your sister, and I have some questions."

"What did she want?" he asked, his voice tinny over the phone.

"She was asking about a vase. She said one of her brothers hid it here."

"Do you know where the vase is?" His tone took on sudden urgency. Ellie traded a glance with Joanna. She didn't know whether Mark was trustworthy either. She decided to play it safe for the time being.

"I've got no idea what she was talking about," she lied. "What's going on?"

Mark was silent for long enough that Ellie began to worry the call had dropped. "It all started with my mother's will," he said at last. "She left a valuable antique vase to Iggy, along with most of her savings. Out of the three of us, Jessie's the one who needed the money the most. I'm not sure what the truth of it is, but she claims our mother promised her she would inherit the vase. While she was causing a scene with the attorney, Iggy took the vase and drove away. He met us the next day and told us he hid it somewhere neither of us would find it, and he wasn't going to retrieve it until we left town. Given Jessie's history, I think he was afraid she was going to try to steal it from him. The next day, Jessie came to our meeting with a story about meeting you and going ghost hunting at the Potters' old house. The next day, Iggy turned up dead. I don't know what happened in between, but if I had to guess, I'd say Jessie put two and two together and realized that your 'ghost' was Iggy breaking in to stash the vase. He must have realized that she was suspicious and

PATTI BENNING

gone to retrieve the vase, only to run into her at the wrong time."

"Why would your brother hide the vase in someone else's house?" Ellie asked. "It seems unnecessarily dangerous."

"Because Iggy was a reckless idiot with a love of theatrics," Mark said with venom in his voice. "The Potters are the ones who originally bought the vase. They gave it to our parents as a wedding present. He must have thought it was romantic, that such a valuable heirloom came full circle, or some such nonsense. He was always hopelessly naive, and it's that kind of thinking that got him killed. You don't fool around with something that's worth tens of thousands of dollars." He took a deep breath. "What did my sister tell you?"

"She didn't say much," Ellie said. "Just that she wanted to come in and look for something."

"I'm sorry she bothered you. Did she happen to mention where she was staying? I'll call the police and give them her location. She's already a suspect in Iggy's death."

"The Marigold Motel, room six," Ellie said.

"Thanks. Oh, and Ellie? If you do see that vase, give me a call, okay?"

Before Ellie could answer, Joanna reached over and ended the call.

"What was that for?"

"You shouldn't have told him where his sister is staying!"

"Look, the police need to be involved either way. There's obviously something going on here."

"But what if he doesn't call the police?" Joanna asked. "What if he goes there himself? You can't tell me that guy isn't at all suspicious."

"I don't necessarily trust him either, but it's his sister for goodness sake. He's not going to..." Ellie trailed off, realizing she had made a dangerous mistake. The fact that they were siblings didn't matter. Their younger brother had already died, and chances were one of them had killed him. If Mark was the culprit, she could have just signed Jessie's death warrant.

CHAPTER EIGHTEEN

"Call her," Joanna said. "Warn her that Mark knows where she is."

"I have to look up the number to the motel. Hold on…"

She turned on the computer screen and searched for the Marigold Motel. With shaking fingers, she dialed the number and asked for room six. The phone rang so many times that Ellie was worried Jessie wouldn't answer. At last the phone was picked up and Ellie was greeted with a staticky "Hello?"

"Jessie?"

"This is she," the other woman said. "May I ask who's calling?"

"It's Ellie, from the pizzeria," Ellie said.

"Oh, Ellie! Did you find the vase?"

The stupid vase again, she thought. *Is that all that matters to them?*

"No," she lied. "I just need to call to tell you that —"

"Hold on, someone's at the door. I think it's the pizza I ordered."

"Wait," Ellie said, but it was too late. She heard the

sound of voices from the other line, and waited what felt like an eternity before Jessie picked up the phone again.

"Your pizza place has really fast delivery," Jessie said. "I tipped your delivery guy a good amount, don't worry. What was it you wanted?"

"I made a mistake," Ellie said. "I told —"

"Hold on, someone's at the door again. The delivery guy must have forgotten something."

Ellie heard a clunk as Jessie put the phone down a second time. She had a bad feeling in the pit of her stomach, and strained to listen. There was silence, then a sudden crashing sound, as if the door had been slammed open. She heard shouting, then the line went dead.

Ellie and Joanna exchanged horrified looks.

"What have I done?" the pizzeria owner whispered. "That was Mark, I just know it."

"Call the police," Joanna said. "Tell them what happened."

"They won't be fast enough," Ellie said. "Let's go, I'll call them on the road. The motel's not far from here."

"Ellie —"

"Look, you don't have to come, but I can't let Jessie get hurt because of my mistake."

Her friend sighed, then nodded. "All right, I'll come

with you. You drive, I'll call the police and let them know what happened."

Ellie rose and hurried out of the home office, then stopped in her tracks and turned around. Her eyes landed on the vase. It was what had started all of the trouble, now maybe it could end it.

She drove as quickly as she safely could while Joanna talked to the dispatcher over the phone. Ellie kept having to cut in to clarify points. She realized how much of a mess the whole thing was. As bad as it was for her, it was a thousand times worse for the three siblings. Her own relationship with her mother and her father might not be perfect, but thinking about these three siblings who were so willing to kill over a valuable heirloom made her realize just how much worse things could be.

She pulled into the motel parking lot while Joanna was still on the phone. Her friend pulled the receiver away from her ear to say, "Wait. We shouldn't go in ourselves. The police are on their way."

Ellie shook her head. "I have to. This is my responsi-bility. I have to make sure no one else gets hurt."

"Ellie —"

The pizzeria owner ignored her friend. She grabbed the vase from the back seat then slammed the car door. She looked at the room numbers and found room six on the bottom floor, located on the far corner of the building. She hurried toward it. As she drew closer, she could see that the door was open a crack.

Ellie paused in front of the door, took a deep breath, then pushed it open, the vase held in her arms like a shield. Her forward motion faltered as her eyes took in the scene in front of her. Mark was standing in the room with his back to the wall and his hands held up in surrender, and Jessie was standing a few feet away from him, pointing a gun at his chest.

CHAPTER NINETEEN

B oth of them turned to look at Ellie when the door opened. The pizzeria owner's eyes flew to Jessie's face.

"What's going on here?" she asked, too surprised to think of anything else to say. She had been expecting to have to rescue Jessie from Mark, not the other way around.

"I've finally realized just how messed up my family is," Jessie said. "What are you —"

She cut off mid-sentence as Mark lunged toward her. Ellie flinched as they wrestled with the gun. In just moments, Mark managed to tear it out of his sister's grip. He pointed it at her as she backed up, their positions reversed.

"Give me the vase," he said, turning his head slightly to speak to Ellie while still keeping his eye on his sister. "Just give it to me, and no one gets hurt."

Ellie gripped the vase more tightly, keenly aware that it was her only bargaining chip. "No," she said. "Not until I know what's going on."

"It's none of your business," he snarled. "Just give it to me."

"It is my business. Someone broke into my house in a sort of reverse robbery and left a twenty thousand dollar antique hidden in a box. I think I deserve to know what's going on."

"It doesn't matter what you think you deserve," Mark said. "I've got the gun, so hand me the vase or someone gets hurt."

"If you pull the trigger or make a move toward me or Jessie, I'll throw this thing to the ground. I don't care how much money it's worth."

She shifted her grip on the vase, ready to make good on her threat. With the police on the way, she knew all she had to do was stall for a few minutes. Thankfully, the threat seemed to give both of them pause.

"What do you want to know?" Mark asked through gritted teeth.

"The story. The real story. I'm guessing what you told me earlier wasn't the full truth."

"I'll tell you," Jessie said. "Just... don't let him shoot me. Please, I don't even care about the vase. I just don't want to die."

"If he tries anything, I'll shatter it," Ellie promised.

Mark made an annoyed noise, but seemed to realize he was trapped. He gestured with the gun. "Go on, then, Jess. Tell us both your side of things."

She took a deep breath. "We went to the lawyer's office the same evening the three of us at your pizzeria. He revealed that our mom left almost everything to Iggy. I... I admit that it hurt, but I also sort of understood it. Mark and I got out of town as soon as we could, but Iggy stayed. He's the one who took care of her after Dad died. He's the one who kept her out of the nursing home when she started getting sick. It makes sense that she wanted to leave him something extra as thanks. When Mark heard the will, he got angry." She hesitated, glancing at the gun. "I'm not going to lie, I was a little bit upset too, but not like Mark. He confronted Iggy in the parking lot and... I thought he was going to kill him then and there. I managed to calm everyone down, and we agreed to meet up the next morning. When we did, Iggy told us he had gone to our mom's estate and he took the vase and hid it somewhere neither of us would be able to find it. I know he was scared that Mark was going to go after it. He might have been worried about me too, I don't know for sure. That vase is worth a lot of money."

"I know," Ellie said. "I looked it up."

"Anyway, there was another huge fight. It ended with everyone leaving angrily, with a promise to meet up again later that night. Iggy said he was going to think about splitting everything with us. That was the evening I went over to your house. I met with my brothers afterward and told them about the weird coincidence I'd just had. The pizzeria owner lived in the Potters' old house and thought it was haunted. I thought it was the neatest thing. I told them all about the experiences you had during the storm the night before. Iggy pulled me aside after and told me that he had been the one to break into the attic. There used to be a tree house in that tree by your house, and he climbed it all the time when he was a kid. When he was thinking of somewhere to hide the vase, that house was the first place he thought of. Iggy said he was going to go back that night and recover the vase, because he was sure Mark had put two and two together." She spared a glare for her older brother. "I'm guessing you did end up figuring it out. You went there that night to get the vase and you ran into him, didn't you?"

Mark frowned at her and gave a single, stiff nod. "You're right about that, but you're wrong about why Mom left him everything. It wasn't because he stayed and took care of her, it was because he was a spoiled brat. He was always the baby of the family, and he always got what he wanted. He didn't stay in town to take care of Mom after Dad died, he stayed here because he got to live in a big house for free, Mom paid for anything he wanted, and he didn't have to work a day in his life. I saw him trying to climb that tree like he used to do when we were kids, and I pulled him down. I didn't go into it trying to kill him, but he hit his head against the side of the house. He fought back and managed to wander off. He must have collapsed just on the other side of the road. I came back a couple of times, but I couldn't find the vase."

"Why did you try to warn me away from Jessie?" Ellie asked.

"Because I didn't want you handing the thing over to her. I knew if she got her hands on it, I'd never see it again. When you called me earlier, I thought you might have already given it to her, and I came over here to get it back, and my lovely sister pulled a gun on me."

"You slammed the door open in my face and I thought you were going to attack me! And I would have shared the money with you even if I had it," Jessie snapped at him. "You're the selfish one, Mark. You're the one who drove Mom and Iggy and me away. Maybe she spoiled Iggy a bit, but he was always a good son and a good brother. You were just a jerk who didn't care about anyone but yourself. You never even visited Mom when she got sick. Why would she leave you anything? You should have been the one to die, not Iggy."

"You know what? I'm done with this."

Mark pulled the slide back on the hand gun. Before Ellie could think her plan through, she called his name and tossed the vase toward him when he glanced at her. "Catch!"

Just as she hoped, he dropped the gun in order to catch the vase. Jessie scrambled to retrieve the weapon and aimed it at him, backing away until she was safely out of reach. In the distance, Ellie heard the sirens. She breathed out a sigh of relief. No one was dead, and the police would be there soon. She considered it a good day.

"So, what's the verdict?" Ellie asked. "Do we have a ghost? Should I invite Jessie back for a seance?"

"Not unless she wants to talk to the leak in our master bathroom," Russell said, turning off his flashlight and coming into the hallway. "Because that's what's been causing all of this trouble. It's situated right above the guest bathroom — it made installing the plumbing simpler — and one of the pipes is leaking. I'm guessing it corroded some wires, which is why the lights kept going out. We're lucky it didn't start a fire or blow a fuse to this whole part of the house."

"That's it? Really?" Ellie groaned and shook her head. "I can't believe I thought a leaky pipe was a ghost. I must be going crazy."

"Not crazy," Russell said, stopping to kiss her. "Just stressed. From the sound of it, you've had quite the week."

"Never go away again," she said. "You keep things sane around here."

He chuckled. "I'm not planning on it, not anytime soon, at least. It's good to be back, even if I missed all of the action."

"I'm sorry you had to miss the rest of your confer-ence," she said, following him into the kitchen. He pulled out the phonebook and began flipping through it.

"I don't care about missing the conference as much as I care about missing everything that happened here." He looked up from the book and frowned at her. "Bethany told me all about it. He had a gun, Ellie. He had a gun and you threw a vase at him."

"A twenty thousand dollar vase," she said. "He killed for it. He wasn't about to let it fall."

Russell shook his head. "You drive me crazy, did you know that?"

"But you love me in spite of it."

"I don't love you in spite of anything," he said, perusing the phone book again. "I love you because of everything. Ah, there's the electrician. We used this guy when we had some wiring problems at the sheriff's department. He's reliable. I'll get him out to fit the lights in the guest bathroom as soon as possible."

"And maybe we should get a heater for that room too. It is kind of chilly in there."

"Really?" He furrowed his brows. "I thought it was too warm, if anything."

"There's a draft," Ellie insisted.

"Coming from where? There are no windows."

The pizzeria owner felt the hairs on the back of her neck rise. Russell was right, there was nowhere for a draft to be coming from. But she *knew* she had felt a chill, and Jessie had felt it too —

No. She forced her mind away from that train of thought. Ghost or no ghost, it didn't really matter. It was silly to be afraid of spirits when the living were so much more dangerous.

"You know, I still have the rest of the week off," Russell said. "Do you want to do something together? Just the two of us?"

She smiled, feeling herself relax. No matter what life threw at her, she knew she could handle it with her husband at her side. They were partners, and there was nothing wrong with wanting him there to face life's trials beside her.

"Sure," she said. "That would be nice."

AUTHOR'S NOTE

I'd love to hear your thoughts on my books, the storylines, and anything else that you'd like to comment on—reader feedback is very important to me. My contact information, along with some other helpful links, is listed below. If you'd like to be on my list of "folks to contact" with updates, release and sales notifications, etc.... just shoot me an email and let me know. Thanks for reading!

Also...

... if you're looking for more great reads, I am proud to announce that Summer Prescott Books publishes several popular series by Cozy authors Gretchen Allen and Patti Benning, as well as Carolyn Q. Hunter, Blair Merrin, Susie Gayle and more!

CONTACT SUMMER PRESCOTT
BOOKS PUBLISHING

Twitter: @summerprescott1

Blog and Book Catalog: http://summerprescottbooks.com

Email: summer.prescott.cozies@gmail.com

And...look up The Summer Prescott Fan Page and Summer Prescott Publishing Page on Facebook – let's be friends!

To download a free book, and sign up for our fun and exciting newsletter, which will give you opportunities to win prizes and swag, enter contests, and be the first to know about New Releases, click here: http://summerprescottbooks.com

Made in the USA
San Bernardino, CA
16 April 2019